cheerful chick

BY **martha brockenbrough**
ILLUSTRATED BY **brian won**

SCHOLASTIC INC.

To Jolie and to Susan, the very best cheerleaders. Bagock! —MB

For Zoe Esther Kanes —BW

Once inside a chicken's nest

A dozen eggs, all Grade-A best,

Lay still and warm, their contents sleeping,

All but one . . .

. . . who came out peeping.

This sunny chicken loved to cheer,

Though grown-ups groaned when she came near.

"She needs to understand we're busy,

And her cheering makes us dizzy."

Cheerful Chick

worked day and night

Until at last her moves felt right.

And then she hatched her lifelong dream
To build a barnyard cheering team.

She got her muscles good and warm
And did her moves with perfect form:

Side splits, wing stands, super punches —

Chicken shook her feathers bunches!

Then, because her dream was big,

She made her pitch to Mr. Pig.

When I say three,
yell P-I-G.

This fellow's jump's
a treat to see!

Mr. Pig, often grumpy

'Cause his slops were cold and lumpy,

Flicked his tail and said, "Shove off.

I'm very busy at my trough."

Chick shrugged her wings. "I bet Ms. Cow

Would like to do some cheering now."

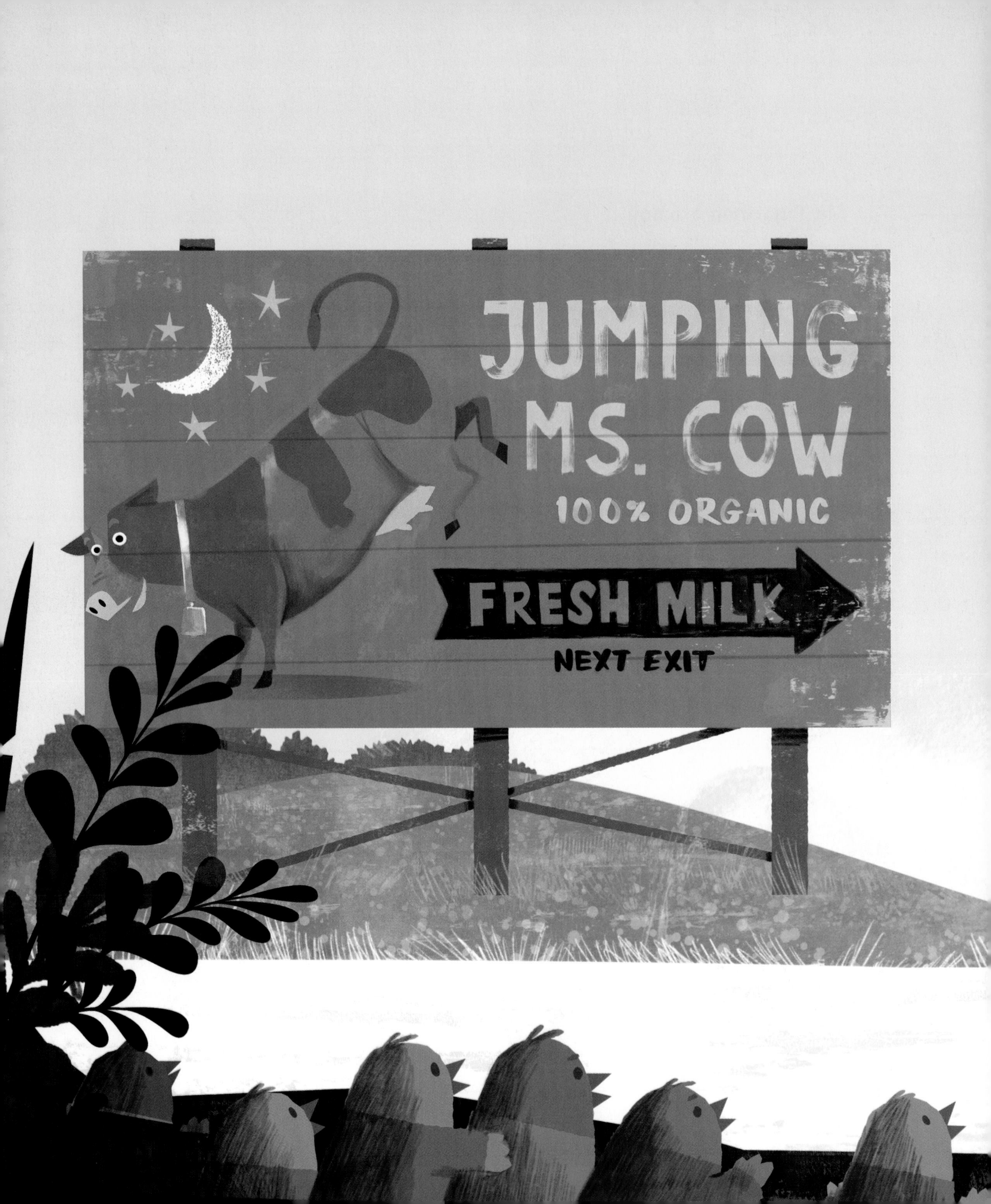
JUMPING
MS. COW
100% ORGANIC
FRESH MILK
NEXT EXIT

Ms. Cow knows all
the wildest moves.

Just watch her stand
on two front hooves!

Ms. Cow just stood and blinked and chewed

And said, "I'm so not in the moooood."

And so, without another peep,

Chick went in search of Mr. Sheep.

Now come on, farm gang.
Don't be drips.

Let's count to ten
as Sheep does flips!

But when she counted, Mr. Sheep

Did not do flips. He fell asleep.

Poor Chicken hung her little head.

Her tiny heart filled up with dread.

In the barn stood one last choice.

She needed time to find her voice.

Now snap your beak
and stomp your feet

'Cause Horse's high kicks
can't be beat!

Mrs. Horse just stared at Chick,

Who felt as though she might be sick.

She touched her wings, as if to pray,

And Mrs. Horse responded . . .

Chick gave it everything she could,

But nothing did her any good.

She chucked her pom-poms in the trough

And then she ripped her sweater off.

'Cause no one cared about her dream.

And no one wanted on her team.

She whispered so that none would hear,

"Who am I if I cannot cheer?"

Chick sat and watched the full moon rise,

And as she did she realized

She didn't need those other folk —

Just wings and legs and lots of yolk.

She gave herself one last routine,

Where every move was strong and clean.

Then something happened as she cheered:

A squad of fluffy friends appeared.

Some cheerful chicks! Eleven more!

(Not that she was keeping score.)

Well, hey now, Horse,
Pig, Cow, and Sheep,
  This farm is full of
  chicks that cheep!

We're two chicks!
Four chicks! Six! A dozen!
  Watch us get this
  barnyard buzzin'!

Since the grown-ups' work was done,

They took part in the cheering fun.

And cheerful Chick knew dreams come true

When chicks do what they're born to do.